In a high-rise building
deep in the heart of a big city
live two private eyes:
Bunny Brown and Jack Jones.
Bunny is the brains,
Jack is the snoop,
and together they
crack cases wide open . . .

This is the story of
Case Number 003:
THE CASE OF
THE PUZZLING POSSUM.

story by
Cynthia Rylant

pictures by
G. Brian Karas

THE HIGH-RISE PRIVATE EYES

The High-Rise Private Eyes

The Case of the
Puzzling Possum

HarperCollinsPublishers

To Bain Wills
—C.R.

To the Chancellor Livingston School
—G.B.K.

Acrylic, gouache, and pencil were used for the full-color art.
The text type is Times.

HarperCollins®, 🎬®, and I Can Read Book®
are trademarks of HarperCollins Publishers Inc.

The High-Rise Private Eyes: The Case of the Puzzling Possum
Text copyright © 2001 by Cynthia Rylant
Illustrations copyright © 2001 by G. Brian Karas
Manufactured in China.

For information address HarperCollins Children's Books, a division of
HarperCollins Publishers, 10 East 53rd Street, New York, NY 10022.
www.harperchildrens.com
Library of Congress Cataloging-in-Publication Data
Rylant, Cynthia.
The high-rise private eyes : the case of the puzzling possum /
by Cynthia Rylant ; illustrated by G. Brian Karas.
    p.   cm.
"I Can Read Books."
Summary: Bunny and Jack investigate the disappearance of a
trombone from Mr. Riley's music store.
ISBN 0-688-16308-4 (trade) — ISBN 0-688-16307-6 (lib. bdg.) —
ISBN 0-06-444316-7 (pbk.)
[1. Animals—Fiction. 2. Mystery and detective stories.]
I. Karas, G. Brian, ill. II. Title.
PZ7.R982 Hq   2001   [E]—dc21   00-030914
❖

10 11 12 13 SCP 10 9 8
Originally published by Greenwillow Books, an imprint of
HarperCollins Publishers, in 2001.

Contents

Chapter 1
Buttons

Bunny collected buttons.

She had a lot of them.

Probably a million.

"Bunny, you've got probably

a million buttons," said Jack

every time he visited.

"Yes," said Bunny proudly.

Jack looked at the buttons.

"Buttons are boring, Bunny,"

he said.

"They are not!" said Bunny.

"They don't *do* anything," said Jack.

"Why don't you collect fun stuff,
like trains?"

"I like buttons better," said Bunny.

"But *why*?" asked Jack.

"Because they're nice and quiet,
unlike some raccoons I know,"
said Bunny.

9

"I'm nice," said Jack.

"You'll be even nicer

if you make me a cup of cocoa,"

said Bunny.

"I can do that," said Jack.

"And I can be quiet too."

"Okay," said Bunny.

RINNGGG! went the telephone.

"If it's for me, I'm not here,"

said Jack. "I'm being nice

and quiet today."

"Ha," said Bunny.

She picked up the phone.

"Hello?" she said.

Jack tried to listen

while he fixed the cocoa.

"*Really?*" Bunny said.

Jack knocked over the milk.

"*When?*" asked Bunny.

Jack dropped a cup.

"*Where?*" asked Bunny.

Jack spilled the marshmallows.

"*Amazing,*" said Bunny.

Jack dumped the cocoa powder.

"Right," said Bunny.

She hung up the phone.

"Jack, what *are* you doing?"
asked Bunny.

"Dropping, knocking, spilling,
and dumping," said Jack.

"Plus being nice."

"Well," said Bunny,

"it's time to go to work.

We have a case."

"Really?" said Jack.

He sat on a marshmallow.

"That was Mr. Riley,

who owns the music store

on the corner," said Bunny.

"Someone keeps taking a trombone."

"Taking a trombone?" asked Jack.

"And putting it back," said Bunny.

"Putting it back?" asked Jack.

"Right," said Bunny.

"We'd better get over there."

Jack stood up.

"Let's have our cocoa first," he said.

"Here's your marshmallow.

Where's mine?"

Bunny looked at him.

"You don't want to know," she said.

Mr. Riley met Bunny and Jack

at the door of the music store.

"Hello, Bunny! Hello, Jack!" he said.

"How are you?"

"*Nice*," said Jack.

Bunny gave Jack a look.

"We're fine, Mr. Riley," she said.

"But how are *you*?"

"Confused," said Mr. Riley.

"In the evening

when I close the store,

the trombone is in the window.

But the next morning it's gone.

Then the next morning it's back.

Then the next morning it's gone again.

Then it's back."

"Whoa, you're making me dizzy,"

said Jack.

"Sorry," said Mr. Riley.

"May we look at your window?"

asked Bunny.

"Sure," said Mr. Riley.

"But the trombone isn't there.

It's gone today," he said.

"But yesterday it was there.

And in the morning it may be back."

"I think I'm gonna be sick,"

said Jack.

"Come on, Jack," said Bunny.

"Let's look for clues."

"Okay," said Jack.
"But let's not talk about
last night and this morning
and yesterday and today
and the next morning,
or I may throw up."
"Right," said Bunny.
"We'll just look for clues."

23

"Oh, I forgot," said Mr. Riley.

"The trombone did show up

for a while yesterday morning,

but then it . . ."

"GOTTA RUN!" said Jack,

heading for the bathroom.

"Oh, dear," said Bunny.

"I'll just have to start without him."

Mr. Riley went back to work,
and Bunny looked at
the display window.
"Hmmm," she said. "A piece of straw."
"Hmmm," she said again.
"Muddy prints."

She wrote down:

1. straw
2. muddy prints

Bunny was still looking

when Jack came back.

"Feeling better?" asked Bunny.

"Bluh," said Jack. "Did you solve it?"

"*Not yet*," said Bunny.

She showed Jack her clues.

"Straw and mud," said Jack.

"Sounds like a farm. Or a barn."

"Or a *hayride*!" said Bunny.

"Where have I seen that word?"
asked Jack.

"On Mr. Riley's door!" said Bunny.

"Come on!"

Sure enough, on Mr. Riley's door
there was a sign for a hayride.
" 'Take a hayride with Gus
and his Big Brass Boys,' " read Jack.
"Brass!" said Bunny. "That's it!"
"Jack," she said,
"we're going on a hayride."

"Just when I was starting

to really like standing still,"

said Jack.

"Don't worry," said Bunny.

"You won't get dizzy again."

"Just don't invite Mr. Riley

to come with us," said Jack.

"I promise," said Bunny with a smile.

Chapter 3
The Culprit

Jack picked Bunny up that night.

He was wearing a cowboy hat.

"Howdy," he said.

"You look like a bandit," said Bunny.

"All raccoons look like bandits,"

said Jack.

"Yes, but the hat makes you look

like a *professional* bandit," Bunny said.

"Goody," said Jack.

"Do you like my boots?"
asked Bunny.

"You look like a rabbit," said Jack.

"I *am* a rabbit," said Bunny.

"Yes, but boots make you look
like a *professional* rabbit,"
said Jack.

"Oh, for heaven's sake," said Bunny.

"Let's go."

Jack and Bunny took a taxi
to the hayride.
"I'll bet we're the only people
who ever took a taxi to a hayride,"
said Jack.
"Maybe," said Bunny.

When they got to the farm,

there were thirty taxis lined up.

"Guess not," said Jack.

"Come on. Let's go look for

Gus's Big Brass Boys," said Bunny.

Jack and Bunny strolled

around the farm.

People were singing and
dancing everywhere.
There was a lot of straw.
There was a lot of mud.
And, up on the hay wagon,
there was one trombone.
"Look!" said Bunny.

A young possum wearing a long scarf
was playing the trombone.

He was very good.

When he finished, everyone clapped.

"That's our guy," said Jack.

"How do you know?" asked Bunny.

"Look," said Jack, pointing.

Against the barn was a trombone case.

It said RILEY'S MUSIC.

"Bingo," said Bunny.

"What do we do now?" Jack asked.

"We'll follow him after the hayride,"

said Bunny. "I'll bet he takes

the trombone back to the store."

"Right," said Jack. "Ooh—*beans*.

Cowboys love beans. Want some?"

"Sure," said Bunny.

"We may as well have fun

while we're here."

"Yee-ha," said Jack.

Chapter 4
Solved

After eating beans, riding on hay,
and saying "yee-ha" a lot,
Bunny and Jack went back to work.
Their taxi followed the possum's taxi
all the way to Mr. Riley's store.

When the possum stepped out

with the trombone,

they nabbed him.

Oh, it was a sorry sight.

The possum cried and cried.

He told them how the hay wagon

had rolled over his own trombone.

How he needed to play music
to support his mother.
How he had to sneak
into Mr. Riley's store
and borrow a trombone.
Jack nearly cried too.
Jack was sensitive.

But Bunny was practical.
"Well," she said to the possum
(whose name was Freddy),
"how about giving trombone
lessons at Mr. Riley's store
to pay for this one?
Then it will be yours to keep."

"Really?" asked Freddy.

"Sure," said Bunny.

"Mr. Riley's a nice man."

"But he might make you dizzy,"

said Jack.

Freddy promised he would talk
to Mr. Riley the next day.
Jack and Bunny said good-bye
and went back to their high-rise.
"Another case solved," said Bunny.
"Want some cocoa?"

"Can't," said Jack.

"I knocked over the milk,

spilled the marshmallows,

and dumped the cocoa powder."

"Hmmm," said Bunny.

"But I sure was *nice*, wasn't I?"

said Jack.

"Very," said Bunny.

47

"Yee-ha," said Jack.

9 d